THE TALE OF

Firefly the
Foal

For Jonathan, Peter and Amy

Text copyright © 1990 Pat Wynnejones
Illustrations copyright © 1990 Sheila Ratcliffe

Published by
Lion Publishing plc
Sandy Lane West, Oxford, England
ISBN 0 7459 1945 6
Lion Publishing Corporation
1705 Hubbard Avenue, Batavia, Illinois 60510, USA
ISBN 0 7459 1945 6
Albatross Books Pty Ltd
PO Box 320, Sutherland, NSW 2232, Australia
ISBN 0 7324 0227 1

First edition 1991

British Library Cataloguing in Publication Data
(Applied for)

Library of Congress Cataloging in Publication Data
(Applied for)

Printed and bound in Singapore

THE TALE OF

Firefly the Foal

Retold by Pat Wynnejones
from Mrs Gatty's 'Parables from Nature'

Illustrated by Sheila Ratcliffe

A LION BOOK

Oxford · Batavia · Sydney

Firefly was a beautiful young chestnut foal. He loved nothing better than to gallop from end to end of his paddock, his mane flying in the summer breezes. There was no one to tell him what he must do or must not do. He was as free as the breeze itself.

And sometimes passers-by from the village would pause to offer him handfuls of sweet clover and windfall apples. His favourite visitor was Frances, the vicar's little daughter. She would scramble over the fence, tearing her skirts and stockings, to bring him pears from her garden and sugar-lumps. She would stroke his nose and clamber onto his back, which she was not supposed to do because it might be dangerous, and anyway he was not her pony. But there, she was a wayward little scamp, her father said!

For three carefree years Firefly enjoyed his freedom in company with his friends, Whitefoot and Silverstar. Then one day when summer was at its height, the farm workers sweating under the August sun, someone slipped a halter over his head and he was led away from the fields and shut up in a stuffy stable.

No wonder he objected! After three years of running where he wanted in grassy pastures, he now had walls around him and rafters above instead of the wide blue sky.

The first thing he did, of course, was to call out for his friends.

'Whitefoot! Silverstar! Can you hear me?' he whinnied.

They too had been brought in for training and were in the very next stable. Soon there was a conversation going.

'So you two are somewhere near. Why don't you come to me?'

'We can't – we're shut in!'

'So am I. I'm very, very angry!'

'So are we! We're very, very angry too!'

'It's disgraceful!'

'Yes', his friends agreed. 'We think it's very wrong.'

'Wrong?' neighed Firefly. 'Wrong? Nay, it's wicked! I won't be shut in! I'll kick the place to pieces!'

In the stable with Whitefoot and Silverstar was a good-tempered Welsh pony known in the village as 'good old Taffy'. But unfortunately Firefly's stable companion was an old white Arabian mare called Egeria, who liked to gossip and grumble. As soon as she saw Firefly's wilful spirit she rattled her halter and broke into the conversation.

'If I were to tell you why you are here,' she began in a dismal voice, 'you would be more angry still.'

Firefly's curiosity was aroused, as well as his hot temper.

'Well, why *am* I here?' he snorted. 'Why am I a prisoner? Tell me that!'

Egeria gave a great sigh. 'It's because the people you belong to want to make you useful – useful to them, that is. Our masters leave us to ourselves for three years, then they get hold of us and, by fright and force, make us learn everything they want.'

'And then?' gasped Firefly.

'Then it depends on who is your master, whether you are treated cruelly or kindly.'

'If I'm treated badly I shall kick, kick, kick!' shouted Firefly, kicking out at the wooden partition, trying to knock down the walls of his stable.

'I won't stay here,' he neighed, 'to be made to do this and that. I'll run away!'

'It's too late for that,' argued Egeria in her mournful voice. 'You can't begin life over again. You'll just have to learn to obey whether you like it or not.'

'No way!' he retorted. 'They shan't teach me! I won't learn! I shall go on kicking!' And he did just that.

Just then the stable door opened and the trainer looked in. He could see how restless and rebellious Firefly was.

'I shall have trouble with this one,' he muttered. He had just seen Whitefoot and Silverstar in the next stable and had found them quiet and placid, for they had been getting comfort and good advice from Taffy.

'The training's hard,' Taffy had said, 'but worthwhile, for life is so good afterwards.' He told them of the fun of galloping over the countryside, of a good feed of corn, a comfortable stable and someone to rub them down at the end of the day.

'Here I am,' he would say, 'as happy as possible, a pet with all the family. Oh! You've no idea how good they are to me – bringing me titbits – bread or apples to take from their hands.'

As a result, Whitefoot and Silverstar soon finished their training and found happy homes where they loved and obeyed their masters.

Poor Firefly did not have the benefit of all this good advice, for Egeria groaned and grumbled and grouched and made out that all human beings were monsters. Egged on by her he only wanted to resist and rebel and kick, kick, kick!

However, he was so handsome and strong that he was soon bought by a young squire who was a fearless rider. Like Firefly he loved to gallop; but he was a hard master, so Firefly did not love him and would not obey him. There was often a battle of wills, but the more he beat him the wilder Firefly became.

At last the squire tired of trying and sold him to the village doctor for his visits. But every time the doctor stopped at a patient's house Firefly became restless and unruly.

'Stopping at one house, then at another,' he complained to himself. 'Never a good run. I, who have galloped over half the countryside with the squire. Kick? Who wouldn't?'

One day, as soon as he was harnessed in the doctor's carriage, he took the bit between his teeth, laid his ears back close to his head and, pulling madly at the reins, dashed full speed down the lane. They were stopped at last by the turnpike gate, where he finished the day's work by kicking the splashboard to pieces.

So the doctor would not keep him and he was sold again. He went from master to master, becoming more and more uncontrollable. The more they tried to break his spirit the wilder he became. Finally his last owner simply decided to sell him to a butcher for horsemeat.

And so it was that on a hot summer day a hardly recognizable Firefly, with his ribs showing and his head down, was standing in the market-place waiting to be sold for slaughter.

'Why is this beautiful animal here? Who owns him?' a bold young indignant voice suddenly demanded from among the crowd.

It was Frances, the vicar's tomboy daughter, now grown into an elegant young lady and a skilful rider. She had loved Firefly when as a foal he ran in the paddock with his friends, and she recognized his markings in spite of his changed appearance. A gentle hand ran over his dusty coat and kind arms went round his neck.

'Firefly! Is it really you?'

He thrust his hot nose into her cool hand, and she laid her cheek against his.

'Oh, my darling' she whispered, 'you shall be mine and I will never let you go.'

She bought Firefly and joyfully took him home with her. Over patient months she fed and groomed him herself and restored his hope. Firefly was saved.

One sunny day in the village street Egeria was surprised to meet a young lady riding a very well-behaved horse and to realize it was Firefly.

'Well, Firefly,' she exclaimed rather haughtily, 'this *is* a change! What *has* come over you?'

'It is love,' Firefly whinnied happily back. 'It is love that has overcome me! My mistress saved me from a cruel fate. I love her and I would gladly do anything she asks.'

The four stories in 'Village Tales' have been re-created from Mrs Gatty's 'Parables from Nature', first published in 1855. Mrs Gatty was a children's writer, and also a keen naturalist, who used stories from the world of nature to illustrate and communicate truths about God and his purposes. Each of the stories has a particular theme, based on a verse from the Bible.

In **these modern** versions, the stories have lost none of their original freshness and charm, and their message is as relevant today as when they were first written.

'The Tale of Firefly the Foal' is about the power of love to change our hearts and wills, so that we show love in return. The theme of the story is based on the words of Jesus to his followers: 'If you love me you will keep my commandments' (John 14:15).